To Mason,
Go Rocky!
Sam Shane

Today's Starting Line-up

Cartoon All Stars

Rocky
Little Guy • Big Heart
Miesville Mudhens

Cartoon All Stars

Hirwigo (Here-We-Go)
Slugging Sensation
Miesville Mudhens

Cartoon All Stars

Hobo Joe
The Sly Slinger
Miesville Mudhens

Cartoon All Stars

Skipper
Gutsy Manager
Miesville Mudhens

Cartoon All Stars

The Bomber
Fearsome Slugger
Red Wing Aces

Cartoon All Stars

Hairball
Hotdoggin' Centerfielder
Miesville Mudhens

Cartoon All Stars

Grumpy
Almost Always Right
The Ump

Cartoon All Stars

Hammer
Keepin' It Real
Grounds Crew

Cartoon All Stars

Bunyan
The Human Toolbox
Grounds Crew

When you a see a hot dog next to a word....

... just look down at the bottom of the page and we'll tell you what it means.

See the answer here.

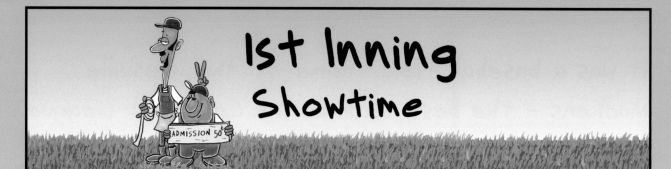

1st Inning
Showtime

One sunny spring day, with a baseball in his pocket and a hoe in his hands, Rocky whacked at weeds in a cornfield. Rocky was the son of a farmer. From sun up to sun down he dug up weeds in that field of corn. But Rocky's heart and dreams were planted in another field on the other side of the fence.

It was a baseball field. Home of the Miesville Mudhens – the best team in the Corn Cob League.

There, next to the fence, stood Hirwigo (Here-we go),
the Mudhens' mighty first baseman, holding a gigantic
bat.

Hirwigo spotted Rocky

"Hey kid, you play baseball?"

"Yes sir!" Rocky answered.

"You know every boy dreams of being a Mudhen!
We're the best team around. If you want to play
with us, you better be good!" Hirwigo let loose
with a thunderous laugh,

"Ha Ha Ha!"

MUDHENS

BA

3

Rocky climbed down the fence and walked over to his big red barn. He pulled the baseball from his pocket, picked up his glove and threw the ball at the barn.

Thwat!!

He scooped it up. Another toss.

Thwat!!

He scooped it again.
"I know I'm good enough
to be a Mudhen,"
Rocky muttered.
"All I need is a chance."

2nd Inning
Draft Day

Suddenly Rocky heard a noise. Waddling from the cornfield was a man with a big belly chewing bubble gum who blew bubbles as big as a balloon.
What began as a baby bubble...

soon got bigger...

The bombastic bubble burst and stuck to the man's face.

Rocky roared at the sticky situation.

"Oops, guess I put too much "X" in the exhale," said the man bashfully.

With gooey gum all over his chubby face the man asked, "Hey kid, what's your name?"

"Rocky."

"Hi Rocky, my name is Skipper, I coach the Miesville Mudhens. I've seen you at our games chasing foul balls. You've got wheels. We could use a fast runner on our team. How would you like to be a Miesville Mudhen?"

Wheels = Quick feet. A person who runs fast.

Rocky's heart almost beat out of his chest.
"Yes sir, more than anything I want
to be a Mudhen!" Rocky said.
"Well, alrighty then!" said Skipper,
"We'll give you a
uniform, but before you play
you've got to pay your
dues. When I tell you to
rake the field, you rake.
When Hirwigo
needs his bats, you
bring his bats.
Are we clear?"
"Yes Skipper," said Rocky,
"I'll do whatever it takes."
"Well then son, welcome
to the club." Skipper blurted
as he blew a bubble and
waddled away.
Rocky's heart pounded.
He was a Miesville
Mudhen. It was his
dream come true.

3rd Inning
Rocky The Rookie

Opening day. The first game of the year. Rocky was a rookie.

"Rocky!" yelled skipper, "Let's go, I need you to rake the field and mow the grass!"

"HEY ROOKIE!" yelled Hirwigo, "Get me my Bats!"

Rocky was paying his dues.

Rookie = A new player on a team.

The Cold Spring Springers came to Miesville for the first game of the year. Rocky took a seat on the bench next to Hobo Joe. Grumpy The Ump yelled,

Hobo Joe was a skinny, smooth, sly pitcher with shaggy sideburns.

Just then Hobo Joe's eyes darted out of the dugout like a laser beam and he yelled,

Hey Hirwigo! Howboutabigrip!!

"What'd you say?" Rocky asked. "I said howboutabigrip. We call it chatter. If you say it slow, it's how-about-a-big-rip. A big rip is a base hit. I want Hirwigo to get a base hit."

chatter = The words players shout to encourage their teammates.

Hirwigo with his big bat and big smile strolled to home plate. He dug into the batter's box. The pitcher for the Cold Spring Springers fired a fastball.

CRACK!

The ball sailed high and deep.
The right fielder raced back
to the fence.
Plop!
The ball fell into his glove.
The Mudhens' fans moaned.
"Holy Moly!" shouted Rocky,
"Hirwigo almost hit
it outta here."
"Yep," said Hobo Joe,
"He almost hit a dinger."
"A dinger?" asked Rocky,
"What's a dinger?"
"A dinger, you know,
a dong, a tater, goin' yard,
jack city, a bomb.
Kid, a dinger is a homerun!"

Dinger = Homerun.

Just then Hobo Joe reached into his pocket and
pulled out a small clump of dirt.
"What's that?"
Rocky wondered.
"This is my
magic dust. It
gives me good
luck."

"Steeeeerrrike Three!!"

yelled Grumpy The Ump. The Springers sprinted off the field and grabbed their bats. Hobo Joe bolted out of the dugout to the pitcher's mound.

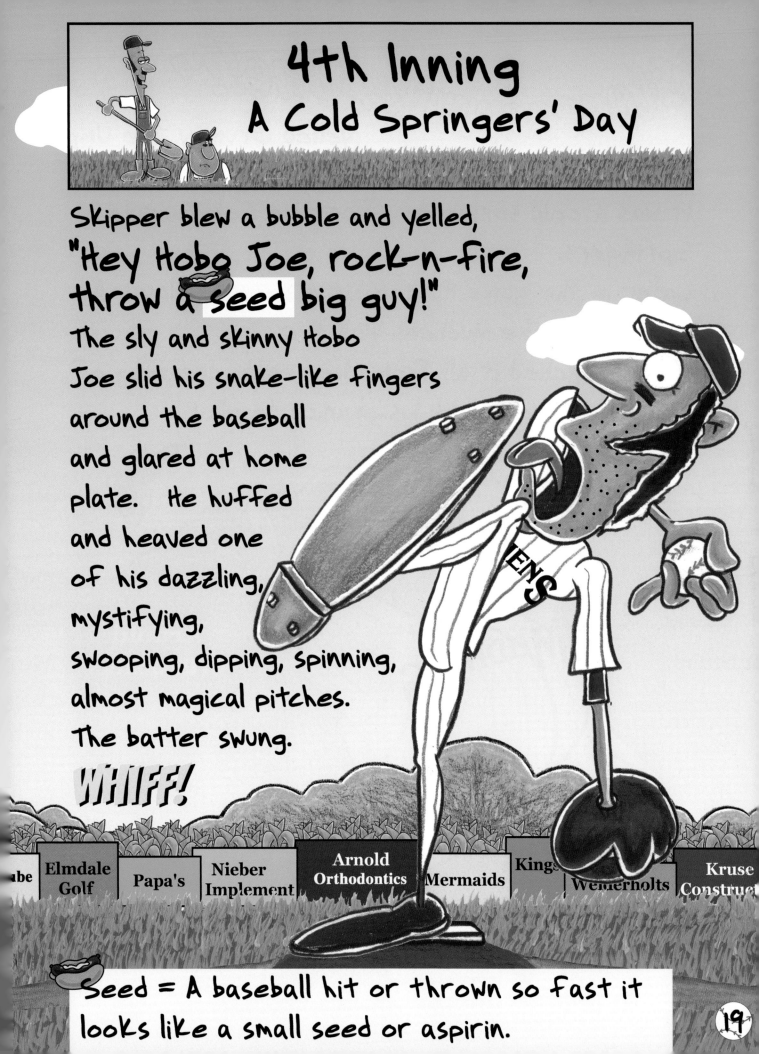

4th Inning
A Cold Springers' Day

Skipper blew a bubble and yelled, "Hey Hobo Joe, rock-n-fire, throw a **seed** big guy!" The sly and skinny Hobo Joe slid his snake-like fingers around the baseball and glared at home plate. He huffed and heaved one of his dazzling, mystifying, swooping, dipping, spinning, almost magical pitches. The batter swung.

WHIFF!

Elmdale Golf Papa's Nieber Implement Arnold Orthodontics Mermaids Kings Weimerholts Kruse Construc

Seed = A baseball hit or thrown so fast it looks like a small seed or aspirin.

"Steeeeerrrike One!!"

yelled Grumpy The Ump.
Then he did it again. And again. And again.
It was a cold spring day for the Cold Spring Springers.
Later in the game Hirwigo hit a booming blast. A big dinger! The Mudhens won 4-0.
Rocky watched it all from the bench, dreaming of the day he would get his chance to play.

5th Inning
The Summer Hummer

As warm spring days turned to hot summer days, the corn grew high above the outfield fence. Hirwigo yelled,

Hey you Mudhens, this is a summer hummer!

The Daily Hen

Mudhens Thrash Royals In Their Own Yard

Visiting the Rochester Royals for the first time this year, the Mudhens rode the back of pitching ace Hobo Joe to an 8-1 win.
Details on page 9.

Hobo Joe gets win

The Daily Hen

Hirwigo Named Styling Slugger of The Year

Mudhens' slugging first baseman, Hirwigo, won this year's Styling Slugger award in the Corn Cob League.
Judges call Hirwigo a true trend-setter for his funky hair style.

Nice hair

Indeed the Mudhens were humming. They had won every game. They hammered the Hamel Hawks and rocked the Rochester Royals.
You see, the Mudhens were a mighty team.

The Daily Hen

Skipper Makes Gutsy Call Miesville Beats Hamel

"I had to make a big gutsy call in today's game. It's a good thing I got a big gut," Skipper said after his Mudhens pulled out a 1-0 win.

Skipper says he has a big gut.

The Daily Hen

Record Corn Crop Expected This Year

Scientists expect a bumper corn crop this year beyond the outfield fence. On a related note, they also predict Hirwigo to cause significant crop damage this year as well.

More crop damage ahead

The Daily Hen

Grounds' Crew Rakes In Awards

After years of feeling like dirt, Hammer and Bunyan won this year's Bad Hop Ballyard Award for their hard work on the field. The two say they'll use their prize money on Gummy Bears and stink bombs.

Gummy Bear Brothers

The Daily Hen

Rocky Pays His Dues

Rocky, the Mudhens' new rookie, has been busy raking the field, lugging Hirwigo's bats and filling the team's water jug. He's living the dream but some wonder if he'll ever play in a game.

Just a water boy?

6th Inning
The Gamer

It was a perfect day for baseball. Rocky had never seen so many fans in the stands. The Mudhens looked mighty. The Bomber and The Red Wing Aces had come to Miesville for the biggest game of the year.

The big game was about to begin when Hirwigo yelled down the bench, "Hey Skipper, we got a problem here."

Hairball, the Mudhens centerfielder, was curled up on the bench like a caterpillar.

"What's wrong?" Skipper asked.

"I don't feel so good Skipper," said Hairball, " I think I ate too many hot dogs. I don't think I can play today."

Hobo Joe looked at Skipper,

"What are we gonna do? Who's gonna play centerfield?"

Skipper stood up,
"Boys, we're goin' with the kid."
All the Mudhens looked at Rocky.
"Son," said Skipper, this is your big chance.
Get loose. You're goin' in."
Rocky's heart pounded. He was scared and excited.
Hirwigo put his big arm around him, "You paid
your dues kid, you deserve it. Now go show 'em
what you're made of."

MUDHENS

27

"Play Ball!"

yelled Grumpy The Ump.
Rocky and the Mudhens ran onto the field.
He couldn't believe it!
He was PLAYING for the Miesville Mudhens!

On this day Hobo Joe had his good stuff. His slider was sliding. His curveball was curving. His splitter was splitting and his fastball was zipping. He was acing the Red Wing Aces.

be | Elmdale Golf | Papa's | Nieber Implement | Arnold Orthodontics | Me aids | Kings | Veiderholts | Kruse Construct

29

Bottom of the third inning. Man on first. No score.

"Hey Rocky," screamed Skipper," Hirwigo's up, you're on deck."

Hirwigo took a mighty swing.

Crack!

The fans jumped to their feet.

"Get outta here!" yelled Rocky.

The ball sailed high and deep over the fence into the cornfield. A sizzling shot that tore through three rows of corn.

The crowd went wild. Hirwigo beamed as he trotted around the bases.

His dinger gave the Mudhens a 2-0 lead.

On Deck = When a player is due to bat next.

"Hey kid, that's what you call crop damage!" bragged Hirwigo as he touched home plate.

"Now it's your turn, go get 'em."

Crop Damage = A homerun that lands in a cornfield and destroys the corn crop.

"**Batter up!**" yelled Grumpy The Ump. Rocky dug in. The pitcher sizzled one right past Rocky.

"**Steeeeerrrike One!!**"

"Geez Louise," Rocky thought to himself, "This pitcher throws gas." The Aces pitcher got an evil twinkle in his eye and sizzled a fastball right at Rocky's chin. Rocky dove for the dirt and rolled around in a cloud of dust.

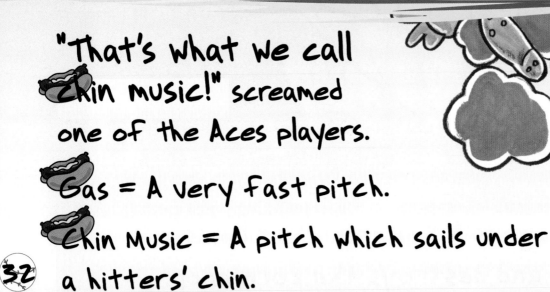

"That's what we call chin music!" screamed one of the Aces players.

Gas = A very fast pitch.

Chin Music = A pitch which sails under a hitters' chin.

Rocky picked himself up, dusted himself off, and dug in. The next pitch zipped right past Rocky again.

"Steeeeerrrike Two!!"

"Okay," Rocky thought to himself, "Get ready to swing this time."

The Aces pitcher wound up again. Rocky was ready. He swung. **Whiff!**

"Steeeeerrrike Three you're out!"

yelled Grumpy The Ump.

With his head hung low Rocky shuffled back to the dugout.

"I'm no good," he thought. "What was I thinking? I'm not good enough to play for the Mudhens."

Hobo Joe walked up to Rocky, "Buck up big shooter. Everybody strikes out in this game. Remember Rocky, we all fail. The trick is to pick yourself up after you fall down. Now let's go out there and win the game. We're counting on you."

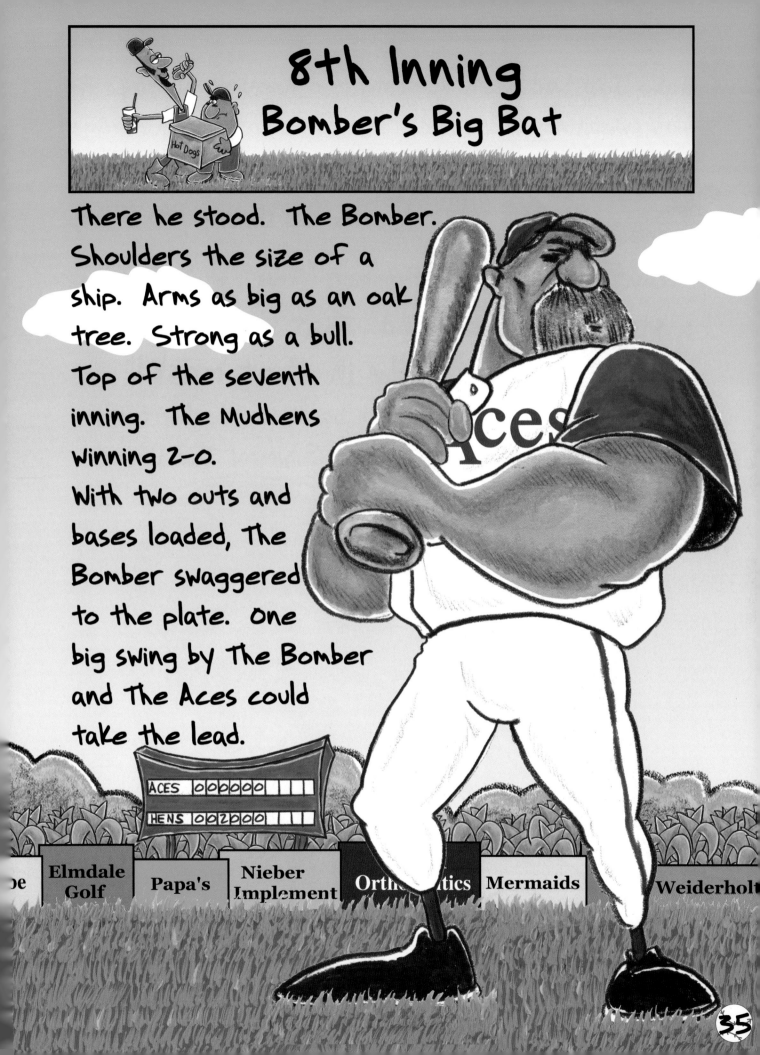

8th Inning
Bomber's Big Bat

There he stood. The Bomber. Shoulders the size of a ship. Arms as big as an oak tree. Strong as a bull. Top of the seventh inning. The Mudhens winning 2-0. With two outs and bases loaded, The Bomber swaggered to the plate. One big swing by The Bomber and The Aces could take the lead.

Hot Dogs

ACES | 0 | 0 | 0 | 0 | 0 | 0 | | | |
HENS | 0 | 0 | 2 | 0 | 0 | 0 | | | |

Elmdale Golf   Papa's   Nieber Implement   Orthopatics   Mermaids   Weiderholt

35

Hobo Joe had been huffing and heaving all day. He was sweating and tired. The fans sat on the edge of their seats. Hobo Joe fired a fastball.

"Steeeeerrrike One!!" screamed Grumpy The Ump.

"What?!" yelled The Bomber, "That was NOT a strike. Are you blind? That was a foot outside! Poke a hole in that mask!"

"That's enough Bomber, get back in the batter's box and let's play ball," yelled Grumpy The Ump.

The ball shot like a rocket toward the clouds.
It got

smaller and **smaller** and smaller.
Rocky could hardly see it. Suddenly it
began to fall right at Rocky!
Then it got bigger...

and bigger....

and bigger...

Rocky missed it.   Three Aces scored and now they
were winning 3-2.
Rocky felt awful. First he struck out and now this.
But for some strange reason Rocky remembered
what Hobo Joe told him.
Sometimes bad things happen.
"Forget it," Rocky thought,
"pick yourself up and
move on."

Larry Schoe
Lawyer

Gorman
Meats

Rocky and the Mudhens had one last chance. Bottom of the ninth. Trailing 3-2, the Mudhens were down but not out.

"Hey guys," said Hairball, "I'm sorry I ate too many hot dogs and got sick. I want to do something for the team. Let's put on our rally caps."

Just like Hobo Joe's magic dust, it gave them good luck.

Rally Cap = A baseball cap turned inside out and often worn backwards for good luck.

At first there was no luck. The first Mudhen
struck out. But then a funny thing happened.
The rally caps started working. The Mudhens got
a hit. Then another hit. Then a walk. Suddenly
the bases were loaded with just one out. And
Hirwigo was up. Hirwigo strutted to the plate
with his big bat and big smile. He dug in.
The crowd cheered.

"Hey Hirwigo, howboutabigdinger,"
yelled Hobo Joe who turned to Rocky and said,
"Kid, you better be ready, you're on deck."

The Aces ace pitcher twisted, kicked and zipped a fastball right down the middle. Hirwigo smiled and watched it go by.

"Steeeerrrike One!!"

yelled Grumpy The Ump.

The next pitch came sizzling right down the middle. Hirwigo took a big swing and barely hit it.

"Foul Ball!"

Hirwigo felt his small nerves tingle just a wee bit. Then the pitcher reared back and did something very sneaky and very clever. He threw a slow, swooping, looping pitch. Hirwigo waved his big bat like a wet newspaper.

"Steeeeerrrike Three!!"

Hirwigo struck out.

WHIFF!

The crowd fell silent. The fans sat stunned. They couldn't believe their eyes.

Now it was up to Rocky.

"Oh no, all we have left is the new kid. All he does is strike out and drop pop-ups. We're doomed," mumbled a fickle fan.

Rocky turned and took a peek at the crabby crowd.

Hobo Joe walked up to Rocky, "Hey kid, don't listen to them. If you listen to them, you have rabbit ears."

Rocky turned to Hobo Joe, "What are rabbit ears?"

"Do you know how rabbits have big ears?"

"Yes sir," said Rocky.

Rabbit ears = When a player listens to and believes bad things others say about them.

"Rocky," said Hobo Joe, "If you have big ears, it means you hear the bad things people say about you. It's not important what other people say about you. What's important is what you believe. Do you believe you can get a hit?"

"Yes I do!" Rocky said.

"Great!" said Hobo Joe, "Then tuck in those rabbit ears and go do it. Oh and just in case, let me give you a little magic dust for good luck."

Rocky stepped into the batter's box.

ssssssssssssssss! POP!

The first pitch sizzled right past Rocky into the catcher's mitt.

"Steeeerrrike One!!"

"It's over," blurted a fan.

ssssssssssssssss! POP!

Second pitch, same thing.

"Steeeerrrike Two!!"

The fans groaned.
Rocky was nervous. But this time he was not scared.
This time he felt something he never felt before.
Rocky began to believe in himself. He realized he could do this.
The Aces ace pitcher reached back and fired a fastball.
Rocky took a rip.

The ball bounced off his bat and dribbled between the pitcher's legs. Rocky ran as fast as he could run to first base. The Aces' infielders darted after the ball as it slithered and squirted through the grass. Rocky ran hard.
The fans cheered.

WHAM!

Two infielders collided and fell to the ground. With Rocky racing to first, the other runners dashed around the bases to home plate.

"Run Rocky Run!" screamed Skipper.
The Aces third baseman swooped in and picked up
the ball. He fired it to first base.
Rocky lunged and stomped down
on first base. He looked up
at Grumpy The Ump.

And...

The crowd roared with delight as two Mudhens scored.

MUDHENS WIN!
MUDHENS WIN!
MUDHENS WIN!

Hobo Joe, Hirwigo, Hairball and the rest of the Mudhens rushed onto the field. Skipper was so excited he swallowed his gum.

Hirwigo threw Rocky on his shoulders.
The crowd cheered.
"I did it Hobo Joe, I did it!"
beamed Rocky with a big smile.
This was even better
than his dream.
Rocky was more than a
Miesville Mudhen.
Rocky was a hero.

Now, with the baseball field quiet, the stands empty and the game over, Skipper, Hirwigo, Hobo Joe, Hairball and Rocky celebrated their victory. They sipped on lemonades.

"Son, you're my hero," Hirwigo said to Rocky. "The best ball players have a big heart. You have a big heart, Rocky. If you love something and work hard at it, then in the long run, you'll win in anything you do."

"And you know what I like the best about it kid?" said Skipper.

"What's that?" Rocky asked.

Skipper looked him right in the eye, "You sacrificed for the team. You paid your dues. That shows commitment. It shows you're dedicated and a team player. The team is always more important than any one player. You're a gamer, Rocky."

Gamer = A player who plays well in big games.

Then Hobo Joe glanced at Rocky with a sly, smooth grin, "I've got another secret for you, kid. Remember my magic dust?"

"Yep."

"Well, it's not magic," said Hobo Joe. "It's just dust. It's dirt. There's nothing magic about it. What you did today you did on your own. The only magic was that you believed in yourself."

"That is s-s-s-o-o-o cool," said Rocky as he gulped down the last of his lemonade. He looked at his new teammates and held up his hand.

"Howboutahighfive!"

Rocky turned and started walking to his farmhouse.
Then Hirwigo hollered,

"Hey Rocky you're still a rookie, don't forget to bring my bats tomorrow."

"Alright, Hirwigo, I'll bring your bats," said Rocky.
As he walked home Rocky knew he was a Mudhen and a hero.
Rocky was very happy.

Glossary - More Baseball Lingo

Blue = Umpire.

Can of Corn = A lazy fly ball which is easy to catch.

Goin' Yard = Homerun.

Boot = When a fielder fails to make a play he should make. Also known as an error.

Ice Cream Cone = When a player barely catches a ball. With half of the ball hanging over the edge of the glove, it looks like an ice cream cone.

Uncle Charlie = Curveball. Also called a deuce or yakker.

Southpaw = A left-handed pitcher.

Ride The Pine = To sit on the bench.

Frozen Rope = A hard line drive hit by a batter.

Meat = An easy pitch to hit.

Band Box = A small ballpark with short fences.

Printed in the United States of America

Designed by Dan Marso

First Edition

ISBN 0-9748922-0-3

LCCN 2004090100

For information on special discounts for bulk purchases
and Rocky The Mudhen merchandise, please contact
Rabbit Ears Press & Co., 551 Valley Road PMB 374, Montclair,
NJ 07043 or visit our Web site at www.rockythemudhen.com
http://www.rockythemudhen.com

Boring

The Authors

Dan Marso and Sam Shane spent most of their summer days in Minnesota on baseball diamonds. They shared the dreams, failures, and triumphs of the game. Today both men have devoted their lives to telling and illustrating stories.

Sam grew up in Hastings, MN. He graduated from, and played baseball for, the University of Minnesota. He is an award-winning journalist who has spent more than 15 years as a T-V news anchor/reporter. Sam is currently an anchor for MSNBC. He lives just outside New York City with his wife Stephanie and their daughter Peyton.

Dan grew up in Mankato, MN. He graduated from, and played baseball for, the University of St. Thomas. He is a cartoonist who named his company, Friday Dog Cartooning, after his dog, Friday. Dan lives in St. Paul.

Acknowledgements

You would not be reading this book had it not been for the advice of many people in our lives. We are grateful to our families and friends who encouraged us and believed in this book. Thanks to the many hilarious guys with whom we played baseball. Their humor, wit, and desire to win inspired us. We also appreciate the cooperation of the many people and players who make Minnesota amateur baseball great. Finally, thanks to everyone who picks up this book and reads it. We hope you enjoy it and we hope it enriches your life.

Special Thanks
Miesville Mudhens
Vince Flynn
Mary Ann O'brien
Tom Nguyen
Charlie Callahan
Shelly Angers
Stephanie

Pick Up A Book / Go Play Catch!

Skipper and the boys can tell you that baseball is a game of inches and numbers. We hope this book will help change a few of the following numbers for the better:

- National surveys show nearly one in five children in America grows up functionally illiterate.
- National surveys show nearly one in eight children in America are overweight.

All of us can do something to encourage our children to read and exercise. A portion of the proceeds from this book will be donated to children's literacy and exercise campaigns.

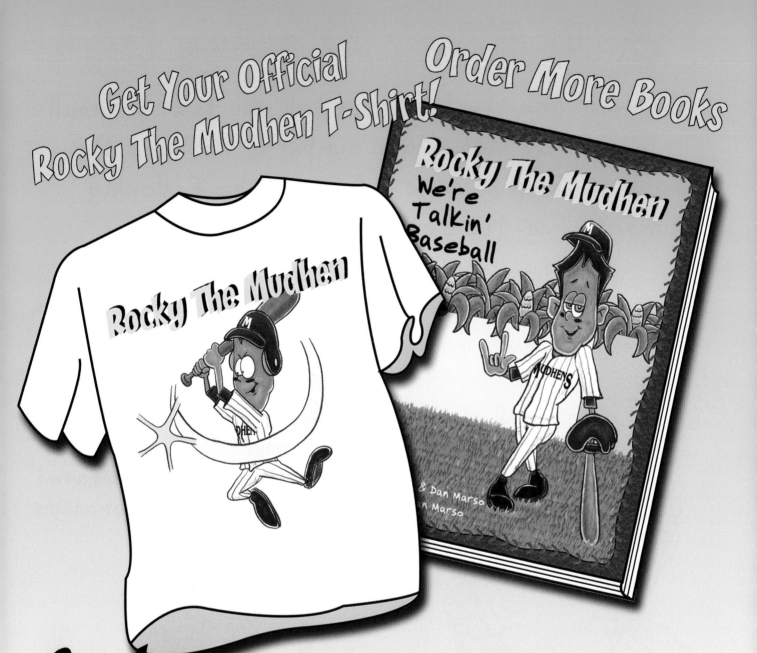

Go to:
www.RockyTheMudhen.com

Or write to:
Rabbit Ears Press & Co.
551 Valley Road PMB 374
Montclair, NJ 07043
(Please include a self-addressed stamped
envelope for an order form.)

"This book will help the reader understand that failure is information that can be useful in improving your weaknesses rather then a threat to your emotional well being and self esteem. A fun read for those who want to learn more about how to overcome your setbacks and gain the confidence to be a success in life."

John Anderson
Head Baseball Coach
University of Minnesota